CARTEL PUBLICATIONS
PRESENTS
MADJESTY
VS.
JAYDEN
WHERE
ARE THEY
NOW SERIES
FROM THE NATIONAL BESTSELLING BOOK: RAUNCHY
T. STYLES

Are You On Our Email List?

Sign Up on Our Website

www.thecartelpublications.com

Or Text the Word: CARTELBOOKS To

22828

For Prizes, Contests, Etc.

Check out other titles by The Cartel Publications

Shyt List 1: Be Careful Who You Cross
Shyt List 2: Loose Cannon
Shyt List 3: And A Child Shall Leave Them
SHYT LIST 4: Children Of The Wronged
Shyt List 5: Smokin' Crazies The Finale'
Pitbulls in a Skirt 1
Pitbulls in a Skirt 2
Pitbulls In A Skirt 3: The Rise Of Lil C
Pitbulls In A Skirt 4: Killer Klan
Pitbulls In A Skirt 5: The Fall From Grace
Poison 1
Poison 2
Victoria's Secret
Hell Razor Honeys 1
Hell Razor honeys 2
Black and Ugly
Black and Ugly As Ever
Miss Wayne & The Queens of DC
Black and the Ugliest
A Hustler's Son
A Hustler's Son 2
The Face That Launched A Thousand Bullets
Year of the Crackmom
The Unusual Suspects
La Familia Divided
Raunchy
Raunchy 2: Mad's Love
Raunchy 3: Jayden's Passion
Mad Maxxx: Children of The Catacombs (Extra Raunchy)
Kali: Raunchy Relived: The Miller Family
Reversed
Quita's DayScare Center
Quita's DayScare Center 2
Dead Heads
Drunk & Hot Girls
Pretty Kings
Pretty Kings 2: Scarlett's Fever
Pretty Kings 3: Denim's Blues
Pretty Kings 4: Race's Rage
Hersband Material
Upscale Kittens
Wake & Bake Boys
Young & Dumb
Young & Dumb: Vyce's Getback
Tranny 911
Tranny 911: Dixie's Rise
First Comes Love, Then Comes Murder
Luxury Tax
The Lying King
Crazy Kind of Love
Silence of The Nine
Silence of The Nine II: Let There Be Blood
Silence of The Nine III
Prison Throne

Goon
Hoetic Justice
And They Call Me God
The Ungrateful Bastards
Lipstick Dom
A School of Dolls
Skeezers
Skeezers 2
You Kissed Me Now I Own You
Nefarious
Redbone 3: The Rise Of The Fold
The Fold
Clown Niggas
The One You Shouldn't Trust
Cold As Ice
The Whore The Wind Blew My Way
She Brings The Worst Kind
The House That Crack Built
The House That Crack Built 2: Russo & Amina
The House That Crack Built 3: Reggie & Tamika
The House That Crack Built 4: Reggie & Amina
Level Up
Villains: It's Savage Season
Gay For My Bae
WAR
WAR 2
WAR 3
WAR 4
WAR 5
WAR 6
WAR 7
Madjesty vs. Jayden (Novella)
The End. How To Write A Bestselling Novel in 30 Days

WWW.THECARTELPUBLICATIONS.COM

MADJESTY VS.

JAYDEN

BY T. STYLES

WHERE ARE THEY NOW series

PUBLISHER'S NOTE:
This book is a work of fiction. Names, characters, businesses,
Organizations, places, events and incidents are the product of the
Author's imagination or are used fictionally. Any resemblance of
Actual persons, living or dead, events, or locales are entirely coincidental.

ISBN 10: 1948373149

ISBN 13: 9781948373142

Cover Design: Book Slut Girl

First Edition
Printed in the United States of America

What Up Fam,

Surprise! This is a little unscheduled pop up treat from T. Styles to her ***RAUNCHY*** Twisted Babies! It's a short story that catches you up on the lives of some of your favorite T. Styles characters. The first release in the, ***'Where Are They Now'*** series is this one, ***"Madjesty vs. Jayden"***.

Let me just say that once again, I am incredibly impressed with the creativity and talent of Mrs. T. Styles! Only someone of her vast skill set is able to create a world and, although we haven't been in that world for quite a few years, can put you right back in it without missing a beat. I appreciate her even more now, since we're in a 'pandemic' and can take our minds off of the virus and immerse it into a book. This novella gave me all the feels of the

RAUNCHY world all over again and I know you will love it and feel it too!

With that being said, keeping in line with tradition, we want to give respect to a vet or new trailblazer paving the way. In this novel, we would like to recognize:

GOD

In the good times and in times of despair, God is able! Thank you, God for your grace and mercy. Thank you for keeping us protected and provided for and continuing to be a fence for our lives and the lives of our families. Continue to let us hear you and keep us faithful and blessed. We ask these things and all things in your son Jesus' name. Amen.

Aight Fam, I'ma let you jump on into this here.

Enjoy and stay safe!

God Bless!

Charisse "C. Wash" Washington
Vice President
The Cartel Publications
www.thecartelpublications.com
www.facebook.com/publishercwash
Instagram: publishercwash
www.twitter.com/cartelbooks
www.facebook.com/cartelpublications
Follow us on Instagram: Cartelpublications
#CartelPublications
#UrbanFiction
#PrayForCece
#Godisable

#MadjestyvsJayden

RAUNCHY

SERIES IN ORDER

Raunchy

Raunchy 2 – Mad's Love

Raunchy 3 – Jayden's Passion

Mad Maxxx – Children of The Catacombs

Kali – Raunchy Relived

Madjesty vs. Jayden (A Novella)

Dear Readers,

This is a SHORT STORY.

And the first part of my *WHERE ARE THEY NOW* series.

Enjoy!

T. Styles ☺

CHAPTER ONE

NEW YORK

The room was dark and smoky...

The luxury suite smelled of expensive perfume, weed and unwashed bodies as Jayden sat in the back, melted into a huge brown recliner fed up with the world. She was watching her girls perform for horny rich men, dressed scantly in outfits that had been worn so many times, it felt as if she were watching a bad rerun.

Time may have passed, and her harem may have changed over the years, but one thing remained consistent. Jayden Phillips was a sex pusher. A female who promoted womanizing and she didn't give a fuck. Nicknamed *Thirteen Flavors* in the past, many of her girls tried to escape her grasp. The lifestyle had gotten old to them, and they wanted relief. They wanted a break. They wanted to be with their families. Some even tried to appeal to her feminine nature by begging for mercy, but she didn't care. She kept them as slaves. Forced them away from their families. And pushed them into lifelong indentured servitude.

Despite being surrounded around feminity daily, she herself grew more masculine over the years. Refusing to wear makeup or sexy clothing unless she had a reason. Even at the moment, with the exception of the gold hoop earrings she dawned, it was as if she was trying desperately to avoid being delicate.

Dressed in grey sweatpants, and a white t-shirt with Gucci flip flops, she was definitely comfortable. But she was also hateful. And bitter. She moved in the world as a woman so selfish, human life had become expendable. And still, there was a whisk of beauty that sat below the surface. In the same area that desperately wanted to be loved.

That desperately wanted to be able to sleep at night.

To forget the many things she'd done. The evil things she continued to do.

Especially to her sister, Madjesty Phillips.

The party was set to end in an hour, and she couldn't wait. Besides, the plan was to get some rest to clear her mind. She already popped two Xanax's and was sipping a martini, knowing that when she finally woke out of her coma like sleep in the morning, she would be boarding a plane.

She was just about to relax when one of her thickest girls jiggled in her direction. "Jay, one of my customers won't leave me alone." Shirley was a tall light skin girl with small tits and a natural ass so fat it appeared to pull her pussy toward the back.

When she approached, Jayden wiped her bone straight long black hair behind her ear. "Did he cash out for more time?" She took a sip of her drink.

"No." She whipped her blonde braids over her shoulder. "I told him the party was almost over since we got the flight in the morning, but he don't care. Should we get Jeff to throw him out?"

She sat her drink down on the floor and looked around from where she sat. "Did you find my phone?"

"No, not yet." She paused. "I been looking for it like you said. We all have. Still don't know where it's at though." She put her hands on her hips. "Um, what about the man? Should I have one of the girls fulfill his needs? He doesn't want me."

Jayden shook her head no. "I'll handle it."

This nigga was blowing her night. The plan for the evening was supposed to be easy but now she felt like fighting. She felt like releasing a few of the emotions that held her hostage on a repeated basis. And so, she rose and swaggered toward him.

Always on duty, her two bodyguards walked behind her, while realizing at the same time that she rarely needed help. "Having a good time?" She asked plainly.

"Oh, I see," Scraggly Beard said when he saw her approach. "I asked for something softer, but I'll take the boss instead." He rubbed his hands together. "Besides, you look like trouble." He went to reach for her until the bodyguards stood firmer at her side.

"Get out." She said simply.

Drunk and out of his mind he said, "Why would I do that? I'm just—." Before he could finish his sentence, she brought down her foot and stomped on his dick, causing him to scream octaves he didn't know were available.

"Get out." She said as she continued to crush.

"Okay, okay!" He raised his hands higher. "Just...just please stop."

She released pressure. "Now."

"Fuck!" He yelled holding himself with both hands, while the guards carried him through the exit by the back of his shirt.

When she turned around, she noticed the remaining men were entertaining themselves despite having ten minutes left. When she looked to the left, she saw all of her girls were huddled in a group, surrounding April, the only white girl of her clan. She was on her cell.

Confused, she approached the scene. "What's going on?" They broke open to allow the boss closer to the center.

April hung up and tossed her phone down on the recliner. Taking a deep breath, she said, "Things are getting bad, Jayden."

Jayden glared and crossed her arms over her chest. "Are you talking about the virus again?"

April nodded yes although she was nervous. Jayden had instructed them many times to avoid any topic about 'the pandemic', and so she was annoyed that it was brought up again.

The women had reason to be weary of her temper. After all, over the course of the years, many were certain that Jayden killed the ones who as she put it, 'phased out'. Only to never see their families again.

"The only reason I'm bringing it up is because of the flights." April said softly. "They're they're..."

"Being grounded," Shirley said finishing her sentence.

Jayden frowned. "What you talking about grounded? We can't leave New York tomorrow?"

"Not on a plane." April said softly. "Not right now."

Jayden turned around and faced the men who were waiting for their ladies to return. She needed to get home for many reasons. So, while the money was always good, staying up top was out of the question. She had plans. She *always* had plans.

Clapping once she said, "Gentlemen, this evening is over."

"But we paid our money and—."

"Everything will be refunded." She said before taking a deep breath. "Even the time you already enjoyed with my women."

The girls gasped, none expecting her to go that far. They reasoned something was on her mind.

"Now get out." When the room was empty, she looked back at her ladies. "Shirley, reserve four vans from the service. We're leaving here tonight."

Jayden was about to search for her cell again when she noticed Shirley was still waiting. As if she wanted to say more. "What is it now?"

"I know we have an event in the afternoon back home but—."

"But what?" Jayden stepped closer.

"But we need to be with our kids. Things are getting crazy."

"*We*?" Jayden looked at the women who were looking their way until Jayden faced them. Quickly they began to gather their things to leave. "I don't recall any of the other women begging to be off."

"Jayden, please. Have a heart. I...I don't know what's going on and—."

"Listen, bitch. You 'bout to be fifty feet deep if you don't get the fuck up out my face and get your shit ready." She pointed across the room. "Because trust me, I don't have any problem dumping you in a hole and burying you alive."

CHAPTER TWO

Jayden was on her bodyguard's phone, in the backseat, as he steered the vehicle. They were on their way home to Maryland and she still couldn't find her cell and so she had to use his instead.

When she got her husband's voice mail once again, she took a deep breath. "Derrick, I'm sorry. I...I don't know what I did this time to make you ignore me but I'm ready to do right by you. Also, if you trying to call me you won't be able to reach me. I can't find my cell. But I am on my way home." She ended the call and handed it to Herco. "Thanks."

"No problem, ma'am."

Fifteen minutes later, Jayden was asleep in the back of the van. She already was a hard sleeper but off the drugs she was impossible to nudge.

Although the girls were together in the other three vans she secured, she wanted to be alone so she could rest. But peace wouldn't last always.

Suddenly the vehicle was struck from the back, sending it spinning out of control. It had tucked itself deep within the woods and stopped inches away from striking a tree. The sound of the second crash caused Jayden's eyes to fly open from her drug induced slumber.

Wondering what occurred, she looked around. Smoke was everywhere. "Herco," she said to the driver, placing a hand on his shoulder. His body immediately folded forward causing his forehead to press against the steering wheel. It beeped loudly. "Herco, are you okay?" She pulled him back into the seat and the sound stopped. "Herco!"

Silence.

Coughing profusely, she pushed her door open and it fell to the ground. Once outside, she felt a searing pain on her left side. She was injured. In an effort to investigate the source of her pain, she lifted her shirt and saw a gash about three inches wide on the side of her stomach.

She needed help.

But first she had to check on Herco a bit more. Rushing to the driver's side door, when she pulled it open, she noticed blood pouring from Herco's exposed skull. His injury was worse than she thought, and this raised her pressure. The problem was many. With the gash on her abdomen she needed to remain calm or she feared she'd lose more blood. And then there was the issue of her reputation. She was a greedy woman and so she was hated by many. Being out in the open was dangerous. She needed to be careful.

Taking a deep breath, carefully she placed her fingertips against his throat. It failed to throb in response.

He was dead.

Holding her side, she quickly moved back to where she sat in the backseat. She was on a mission to find his phone to call for help. After a few minutes, she located the device. The screen was mostly crushed but it turned on. The problem was that the phone was locked. She tried so many times to enter a code that before long, she was blocked from all access.

"Fuck!" She yelled tossing it on the ground. From where she stood, she looked through the trees up a hill and could see cars whisking up and down the road. "I gotta...I gotta get some help."

Before making any moves, she raised her pants leg, looked and dropped it quickly. Her small gun was in position.

Even if she walked toward the road, how would she get home? At the same time there was no use in staying by the van. It was hidden from the highway. Away from help. Slowly she walked up the hill, and then through the trees, until she reached the road. Each step she took, she left a puddle of blood along the way.

Once she was on the highway, she saw that a second car crashed. Something told her to walk in the opposite direction, with traffic. As she continued her hike, cars continued to whisk up and down the highway before a white Mercedes drove slowly at her side.

Eager to get assistance, like a madwoman, she flailed her arms wildly. “Help me! Please. I’m hurt! Please!” At first the driver appeared to be slowing down and then suddenly it sped away quickly.

She would do this fifteen more times, until it was clear that no one would stop to pick up a stranger on a dark road, well after midnight, during a pandemic. Still in pain, she decided to walk as far as she could, until she reached an establishment. Once there the plan was to call her husband. Maybe he would take the hike from Maryland to drive her back home.

Maybe.

She hadn't heard from him and it was odd.

After realizing she was expending more energy walking, she decided to try one more time to get a ride. When she did, a silver and dark blue *1977 Ford LTD* pulled up. Releasing a sigh of relief, she lowered her height and hung in the passenger window. An awkward smile on her face. "Thank you for stop—."

What she saw next shocked her to the core.

The driver was her sister, whom she hadn't seen in over five years.

Madjesty Phillips.

Time may have passed but some things remained the same. Sure, Madjesty had a line or two on her face. Sure, she traded her long curly hair for red dreads that curled and loc'd at the same time, creating a *mermaid loc* effect. She was even still dressed as a boy, a cap halfway over her eyes, a white wife beater and green fatigues respectfully.

But the intense look she possessed was unaged.

She appeared deep in thought and slightly innocent at the same time.

There was also a white heavy-set older woman in her sixties in the backseat. She had kind eyes and an open face. After peeping the grey baggy jeans and oversized black New York t-shirt, Jayden believed she was lesbian.

"You need a ride?" The elderly woman asked.

Jayden's heart rocked. Everything about this was off and she had reason to be weary. It was all too coincidental. The last time she saw her sister's face, Madjesty and Kali showed up to her grandfather Rick's house. All because in greed mode, Rick had Madjesty and her son Cassius kidnapped and almost buried alive, because his son put Mad's name on a half a million-dollar life insurance policy and he wanted the money for himself. This did nothing for Mad and Jayden's already tense relationship.

Then there was the past. The story of how the sisters came to be was definitely complex and dark. Their mother, Harmony Phillips, during one of her many whorish episodes, had sex with Jace and his friend Kali on the same day. Causing one of the most uncommon occurrences in existence. It was called heteropaternal superfecundation. One pregnancy. Two different fathers. Back then Kali didn't want to be a father but Jace stepped up where he could.

Years later, after Jace died due to Harmony infecting him with HIV, he still wanted to do right by the girls by making them beneficiaries in his life insurance policy. But this gift would come at a great cost to Mad. It would mean the kidnapping of herself and her son. Luckily, her biological father Kali saved them both and murdered Rick for his efforts. Through it all, one mystery never became clear to Mad.

Was Jayden also involved?

"Madjesty, how did you know I was here?" Her long hair blew in her face and she wiped it away.

"Mad. My name is Mad."

"I'm sorry, Mad." Jayden looked down at herself.

Now she felt dumb dressing down. Because she would never have wanted her to see her like that. After all, Jayden liked to put on airs when necessary.

Madjesty, still cooler than ice in front of a blowing fan, sat deeper into the cream-colored seats of the classic car. "Are you getting in or nah?"

What other option did Jayden have? Sure, she could have refused. Sure, she could have attempted to take the hike to nowhere on her own. But the curiousness of it all had her wanting answers.

So, she accepted the ride and eased inside the butter colored leather interior.

Madjesty drove silently for ten minutes until Jayden decided to speak. "Just so you know, I don't usually dress like this." She combed her long hair down one side of her face with her fingertips, so her sister couldn't see her eyes. "I was just at a meeting."

"A meeting huh?" Mad adjusted her cap a bit more by tugging it down. The car smelled like vanilla.

Jayden raised her chin higher. "Yep. I just bought an apartment building. It was something light and I threw on what I could find."

"In New York?" Mad said sarcastically. "You must be making big money huh?"

She felt like she didn't believe her. *Why didn't she believe her?* When Jayden looked down, and saw a spider on her leg, she quickly brushed it off and stomped it a few times. She figured it must've caught a ride with her from the outside.

"You aight?" Mad asked calmly.

Jayden raised her chin higher. "Yes...there was a piece of lint on my leg."

"It looked like a spider to me." The elderly lady said easing up in the backseat. "It must like you."

Jayden was embarrassed to be caught in such a stupid lie. "Oh, maybe it was."

"It was." The woman said, sitting back in her seat.

Clearing her throat, Jayden said, "Uh, Mad, I've been looking for you over the years. Where have you, I mean, where have you been? I know you moved from where you were staying and it threw me off. It was like you up and left everything and everybody."

She smiled. "I did move. That's right."

"She doesn't like many people." The elderly woman said. "She likes her peace. Ain't that right, Mad?"

"You know it." Mad's eyes appeared to light up when the woman talked to her and Jayden felt a seed of jealousy. Why couldn't her sister look at her the same?

Curious, she looked back at the elderly woman. "Your name?"

She smiled. "Tatio."

She nodded. "Tatio, where are you guys coming from?"

"Why does it matter where we came from?" Mad said. "All that matters is where we going."

Jayden sat back. "Um, you got a phone I can use, Mad?"

"Nah."

Jayden turned toward Tatio. "What about—."

"She ain't got one you can use either."

Jayden's heart rocked as Madjesty continued to pilot the car in what was starting to be thick traffic. It was obvious that many people were fleeing the city to go to safer places, due to the virus. "Well I won't be a bother, Mad. You can actually drop me off at the next business. It can be a store or—."

"A pandemic is going on. If I drop you off, you'll never get to where you going. Trust me, I got you."

The only problem was this...she didn't want her to see where she lived. And then something dawned on her. Mad never asked where to take her. "You know where I live?"

Mad grinned. "I do."

Jayden's face grew hot to the touch. "Are you going to hurt me?"

Mad adjusted her hat. "We hurt each other enough for a lifetime, haven't we?"

"You didn't give me an answer."

"I think I did."

CHAPTER THREE

They had been on the road for an hour when Mad's phone rang. She looked over at Jayden, removed it from her pocket and answered. Taking a deep breath, she said, "*Yeah. I know.*" She turned the radio on and when she heard the news speaking about the crisis, she changed the station to smooth jazz instead. "*I can't do that right now.*" She said in a lower voice on the call. "*I'll let you know.*" She ended the call and tucked the phone in her pants.

"Is everything okay, Mad?"

"Outside of the pandemic?"

"You know what I mean." She sighed. "Please, talk to me. I'm trying to be calm, but I don't...I don't..."

"Trust me." Mad finished. "Things will be cool."

Jayden nodded. "The thing is, I don't trust you."

Mad shook her head softly. "That's funny. Because I've never given you any reason to distrust me."

Jayden frowned. "Wait, are you serious?"

Mad shrugged. "Yeah, I am."

"Okay, since you wanna go there, why did you do it?" She threw her hands up.

Mad looked at her and bypassed a tractor trailer on the left. "Do what, Jay?"

"Rape me?"

Mad looked at Tatio through the rearview mirror and leaned to the left in her seat. It was obvious that the embarrassment of what she'd done as a child still stung. "We talked about this before."

"Did we?" Jayden positioned her body so that she could look at her closer.

"Yeah, we did."

"Well maybe it...I mean...maybe it never sat right with me." She wiped her hair out of her face. "You never gave me an answer I can understand." She folded her arms. "So why did you do it?"

Mad sighed long and hard. "For starters your boyfriend Shaggy raped me in front of my girlfriend." She glared. "And when I was committed to that institution, you never came to see me. We were twins and you abandoned me." She shook her head and allowed a smile to rise and then fall quickly. "Back then, there was nobody in the world more important to me than you." She looked at her. "And that was my greatest weakness."

"It's not my fault that you were committed, Mad."

"Nah, you right. When I cut off my breasts after he raped me, they committed me." She tugged at her cap and thought deeper about the dark day.

"Niggas kill me. Like raping somebody will make them wanna be with 'em. The theory flawed as fuck." She looked at Jayden and back at the road. "But I needed you back then. And you still didn't give a fuck."

"So, because they hurt you, you choose to rape me instead? I'm your sister. Don't you get how fucked up that is? Even now?"

"Our mother was a whore. We're twins with different fathers. Everything about our lives is fucked up. But when I did what I did, I was a different person. And I wanted you to feel what that nigga made me feel."

"Is that why you reached an orgasm too?" She lowered her head. "Because I will never, ever, forget the sound you made in my ear."

Mad grinned. "I know what you're doing, Jayden. And it won't stop what happens next."

Tatio laughed softly and Jayden looked back at her.

At that time Jayden's heart rocked as it became clear they knew something she didn't. "I didn't have you and Cassius kidnapped. I know you think I was involved but I wasn't. My grandfather made the move without my knowing. And I..." Suddenly she remembered her nephew. "Wait, where, where is Cassius?"

"Why?" Madjesty asked shaking her head softly.

"Why?" She repeated. "For starters, I think about him all the time. And whether you want to admit it or not, I took care of him. I—."

"You hid him from me. Pretended like he was yours."

"Hid him?" She yelled. "I saved him after you let some crack whore named Arizona steal him from you!" She pointed. "Had it not been for me you would've never seen him again. Don't just remember the parts that make you look like a victim."

Mad was tickled at her anger but chose to remain calm. "I was unconscious after giving birth to him. Didn't even know my body...could make a baby. When he was born, they snatched him from me. I never saw his face. But none of it matters anymore, Jayden." Mad smiled. "And I know you like to bring up the past. To rock me. But things are different now. I'm different." Mad had always been dark, but the mystery she possessed in the moment, along with the years gone by made her appear more ominous.

Jayden looked down at her bloody shirt and back at Mad. "What's going—."

"I got a text message, Mad," Tatio interrupted. "I think we should go a little faster."

"Faster to where?" Jayden asked.

Mad nodded and sunk deeper in her seat. Looking at Jayden she decided to change the subject. "My wife killed herself. Did you know that?"

Jayden's eyes widened. "No, I'm, I'm so sorry to hear that."

"Are you?" She asked, before speeding a little when she saw the traffic open up a bit, making more room on the road.

"Yeah... I mean...who is she? Or, who was she? Your...your wife?"

"I married Everest." She glared.

The name was familiar. "I knew you guys were together, but I thought it was a...you know...phase."

"It wasn't." She frowned. "Was as real for me as it was for her." She breathed deeper. "Anyway, she took her own life."

Jayden frowned. "That's hard to grasp, Mad. I mean, why would she do that?"

"Let me back up a little." Mad dipped into the glove compartment and grabbed a pack of cigarettes. Removing one from the slot, she lit and pulled. "My wife was blind. Lost her eyesight in a shootout. A bullet pierced her left eye. And fragments took out her right eye too. So, she was afraid to even move around in life." She blew out smoke. "To even get up unless I was at her side. Me and my other son Pickles were her only protection."

Jayden's eyebrows rose. "You have another son?"

"He's like a son to me. Met him in the Catacombs."

Jayden turned her head and rolled her eyes. She always felt like Mad had a tendency to make families on the fly. Which in her opinion made her, emotionally-vulnerable. "I'm sorry to hear that."

"I wish you stop saying you sorry." She glared. "Because your voice tells me you aren't." She breathed deeply. "Anyway, I was just getting her stronger. I was just able to prove to her that I would never leave her side. And then what happens? I was kidnaped."

"Mad, I—."

"And she killed herself." She looked at her with rage. "Because she thought I would never come back. Once again, just being related to you, fucked up my life. So, tell me something, Jay, whose fault was that?"

"She was pretty too." Tatio said to Jayden out of the blue. "Like, really pretty. Like a model but better."

"Tat-tat, put in your earphones." Mad said looking at her through the rear-view mirror before tossing out the cigarette.

While she stuffed her ears with Airpods, Jayden watched the stranger a bit closer in the backseat. It suddenly became obvious that something may have been mentally wrong with Tatio. And she wondered what started the connection between she and her sister.

"My wife's dead but instead of staying down long, I realized I had shit to do." Mad continued. "Things to do."

"Like what?"

Silence.

Jayden felt the burning sensation of the gash on her stomach, which was getting worse. The only relief was that she wasn't losing more blood. "What do you have to do, Mad? Talk to me."

Mad's phone rang. She looked at the screen and then at Jayden. "I'm stopping at the next rest stop."

"Okay, but is everything cool?"

"Couldn't be better."

Jayden exhaled quietly. She figured with the car stopping soon, she could escape, call her husband and save her own life. Because something told her that Mad meant her great harm at the moment and she had to get away.

CHAPTER FOUR

Jayden dosed off. She hadn't planned on getting any rest in her sister's car, but she did anyway. Scared she'd been caught slipping, she was so nervous she popped up and strained her neck. The first thing she did was look at Madjesty.

"How long I been out?" Jayden asked yawning.

"Your bleeding slowed down a little." Madjesty responded.

Jayden looked down at her now bandaged wound. Her eyes flew open. "When did you, when did you do this?"

Mad smiled. "I didn't. Tat-tat did. Said she saw you were hurt. We had some stuff in the glove compartment and that's that. You're all patched up. Still sleep like a log after all this time. Very dangerous."

"But, why? I thought you were mad at me."

"It doesn't matter. I need you alive."

Jayden frowned. She felt it was better to skip the subject. "I'm married." She raised her head proudly. "He loves me a lot. Don't know if I told you. Or even if you knew already."

Mad leaned to the right and looked at Tatio from the rearview mirror. They both shook their heads. "Married huh?"

"Yep. A couple weeks ago."

She nodded. "You know, I never saw that move coming. With you getting married. Ever."

Jayden frowned. "Why you say that?"

She shrugged. "Because to tell you the truth, you don't seem like the marriage type. I mean, you still holding up in the looks department but..."

"Mad, men find me attractive."

"I never said they didn't. I guess what I'm saying is, you basically harder than me these days." She chuckled once while looking at her sweatpants. "Look at how you're dressed."

Jayden frowned. "You don't have to be mean, Madjesty. I know I don't look my best right now, but I always put on gear when I'm home." She looked down. "You should, you should see my life. I have a beautiful home. And a husband who cares about me. Who can't keep his hands off me." Her voice lowered. "I'm happy now."

"Whatever happened to Cliff?"

Her eyebrows rose. "How did you know about him?"

"I know more than you think about *that* ex-husband. I know he's dead too. From what I hear, you had everything to do with that."

Madjesty pulled over and parked on the shoulder. She adjusted the rearview mirror so that she could see in the back window. "Tat-tat, make the call."

"I thought we were going to the rest stop?" Jayden said.

"Chill." Mad advised.

Tat-Tat got out of the car and paced on the shoulder as she talked on the phone, causing Jayden's antennas to go up even more.

"Mad, I really gotta get to where I'm going. I don't mean to be rude but you doing all of this right now is throwing off my life."

"Not much longer, Jay."

"Not much longer for—."

Tatio popped out her Airpods, opened the door and jumped inside. "They pulling up now."

Afraid, Jayden moved to open the door to make an exit. She had enough of the mystery and the games. "You know what, I'm getting out of—"

Tatio slammed a heavy hand on her shoulder and placed the barrel of a gun against her head. She didn't even know she was packing. "You're pretty too. Just like Everest. Did I say that already?"

"Please let me go." Jayden trembled.

"Nah," she continued. "I want you to stay awhile. Mad does too."

Suddenly, to Jayden, Tatio didn't seem as green as she thought. Focusing on her sister she said, "Mad, you scaring me. Please tell me what this is all about. Stop fucking with my—."

"They here!" Mad said looking through the rearview mirror. She pushed her car door open and greeted three people in the vehicle pulling up in the back.

With her sister gone, Jayden thought about making a move again. There was one problem. Every essence of Tatio's being was zeroed in on her. Slowly Jayden's eyes rotated from the side mirror and then Tatio's hand on her shoulder. She felt trapped.

When she looked in the mirror again, she saw the car hazard lights flashing on Mad's face, as she talked to a thirteen-year-old and a thirty something year old. Another man remained behind the wheel. She knew the older male as Krazy K. One of Mad's friends from Mad Maxxx. And she felt they were nothing but trouble.

"Tatio, so, how did you meet Mad?"

"She saved me." She said smiling.

"O...okay, tell me more about it." She swallowed the lump in her throat.

"I was living outside. Spent most of my time in front of a liquor store. With my uncle. She used to come to the store for cigarettes and give me and my uncle food. When he died, she let me stay with her in her big house because she's nice like that." She lifted her hand off her shoulder but maintained the aim of the gun in her direction. "Does a lot for people like me."

"I'm sorry to hear about your uncle." She said, still looking at Mad and Krazy in the sideview mirror. They were in a heated discussion, but she couldn't make out what was being said. "How did he die?"

"I killed him when he was on top of me."

Jayden's heart dropped and she turned her head toward her slowly. "He...he...raped you?"

"Was raping me. And beating me in the head. All my life. I ain't think it was possible for him to get his dick up anymore since he was so old. But he always could."

"How old was he?"

"Seventy-five." She paused. "I told Mad what he'd been doing to me one day, when she was hanging out in front of the store with me. She said I didn't need to put up with it no more. And I believed her."

Jayden swallowed the lump in her throat. "How did you do it?"

"A bullet to the head. He went quick. Like Mad said he would."

The passenger car door opened and Krazy pulled Jayden out of the front seat and stuffed her in the middle of him and Tatio. The car behind him pulled off with the thirteen-year-old, just as Madjesty reclaimed her position in the driver's seat.

"Fuck is going on, Krazy?" Jayden yelled.

"Hello to you too." He grinned evilly.

"I need somebody to tell me something right now before I go off!"

Mad, Krazy and Tatio laughed and this annoyed her even more.

"Mad, I'm your sister." Jayden continued as Tatio maintained the weapon that was trained on her. "And you don't do family like this!"

"Jayden, you are family." Mad pulled into traffic. "I get it. But that stopped mattering a long time ago, don't you think?"

"Why do you hate me so much?" She tried to force out tears and per usual, bring up the past to throw her twin off. "I did what you wanted me to do when you asked for custody of Cassius back. Even though you lied and said you would let me visit him, only to stop me from keeping a relationship with my nephew."

"Is that why you had me kidnapped?"

"Stop it, Mad."

"I ain't want you seeing him no more because he told me you told him to call you ma. And I couldn't have you undermining me."

"So, you take him from me? When you knew how much that little boy loved me?"

Madjesty smirked. "Sometimes you have to do what you have to do. And I realize that it's easier said than done. Especially when you care about someone." She sighed. "But I don't ask questions anymore. I just act these days."

Madjesty's phone rang several times and she looked back at Tatio and Krazy.

"Don't worry," Mad told her friends, avoiding the call. "Things will be fine."

Krazy and Tatio looked at one another as if they didn't believe her.

"Can I ask you something, Mad?" Jayden said. "Since it's obvious you're being secretive on purpose."

"What is it?" She leaned to the left.

"Did you...did you hit the van I was riding in?"

"No."

"So how did you know I was there?"

"I knew you were there because of you. All of this is because of you."

Jayden frowned. "Because of me?" She yelled. "Are you fucking kidding me? I knew you used to be crazy, but I thought you'd grow the fuck up by now! We haven't spoken in years. Haven't even seen your face. So how could it be because of me, bitch?"

QUICKLY, Tatio elbowed Jayden in the jaw, causing blood to fly from her mouth. After the blow, her head rocked to the right.

"Aye, easy, with that shit," Krazy yelled at her. "Her head almost bumped into my mouth."

"I'm sorry...I'm sorry."

"She hit me in the fucking mouth!" Jayden yelled. "What the fuck, Mad! You gonna let her do this to me?"

"Aye, quit all that hollering before she do it again." Krazy responded.

Suddenly Tatio got upset and began hitting the sides of her head with her free hand. "I went too far. I went too far. I went too far. I went too far. I went too far. I went too far."

"Aye, Tat-tat, she fine." Mad said while still steering the car. "Be easy."

"I went too far. I went too far." She continued to slap at her skull.

"Aye, Tat-tat, chill the fuck out!" Krazy said.

"I went too far...I went too far...I went too far."

"Tatio, Jayden is fine!" Mad said a bit louder looking at her through the rearview mirror. "Now stop hurting yourself." She looked at her sister from the mirror. "Aren't you fine?"

Jayden felt like she was dreaming as she held her bloody mouth. Everybody around her appeared insane. "What is happening?" Jayden whispered. "Where the fuck am I?"

Madjesty pulled the car over and turned around. As Tatio continued to slap herself in the face.

"Are you fucking fine or not?" Mad yelled at her sister.

Jayden wiped the blood from her mouth on her sweatpants. "Yeah, Mad. I'm fine."

"Then tell Tat-tat."

Jayden looked at her and took a deep breath. She planned to have the woman killed before the week ended. "I'm fine, Tat-Tat. No need to hurt yourself."

Only then did she stop laying hands on her own face.

Madjesty was about to pull back into traffic until Jayden said, "I have to go to the bathroom."

"It can wait." Madjesty pulled down on the gear shift.

"Please! It's...it's bad." She shook her right leg rapidly.

She put the car back in park. "Well you better make it quick. There isn't much time."

CHAPTER FIVE

Mad's car was pulled on the shoulder of the highway. While she was inside the car on a heated call, Tatio escorted Jayden to a piece of grass to urinate. Krazy, on the other hand was messing with the trunk of the car as vehicles whizzed by on the highway.

"You can go right here," Tatio said as she and Jayden stood close to the bushes. She was holding her arm. They received a few stares from drivers, but most were on their way to somewhere other than New York. And so, nobody cared.

"Can you get off of me?" Jayden yanked away.

"I can't leave you." She grabbed her elbow again. "Madjesty told me to keep my eyes on you so that's what I'm gonna do."

"What is your thing with my sister? I mean, do you like her or something? Because all of this is bizarre."

She glared. "You betta make it quick." Tatio looked at Mad who was staring in their direction. "She's calm now, but I've also seen her angry. And you don't want that."

"Okay, well, um, can you turn around at least?" She paused. "Please."

She released her hold. "Alright, but you gotta hurry."

"I'll be quick, besides, where am I gonna run?"

Tatio looked down and slowly turned around. Jayden pushed her sweatpants down and then her panties. Pretending she was about to squat; she took off running instead.

"Oh no!" Tatio yelled as she ran after her. "Why did you do that?"

Jayden was quick as her sneakers crunched against the gravel. Her sweatpants hung down her ass and she almost got away, until her back was weighed down by Krazy. "You shouldn't have done that shit." He yelled. "Causing a fucking scene and shit."

"I had to use the bathroom."

"So, you run?" He lifted her up and grabbed her by the arm as she pulled up her pants. "You only making things worse for yourself in the long run." He continued as he yanked her toward the car.

"Making what worse?" She looked at him, hoping he'd reveal something to her. "Why am I making it worse?"

"It doesn't matter. I never fucked with you. Never liked how you did Mad when we were kids. And I wish everything terrible you got coming your way."

"What is coming my way?" She yelled. "At least fucking tell me that. What's with all the secrecy?" As he walked her to the car, she saw a scratch on the front bumper. Did Mad lie and bump the van which caused an accident?

I knew you hit the van, bitch. She thought to herself.

"Krazy, I gotta pee." She continued.

"Pee on yourself. You shouldn't have tried to be slick." He yanked the door open and stuffed her in before crawling inside with her.

"That was stupid, Jay," Mad said, placing the car into drive, before pulling off the shoulder. "Real fucking stupid."

"Why did you lie, Mad?" She yelled, whipping her hair out of her face.

"Lie about what?" She merged into traffic.

"You did hit the van! I saw the front of the car!"

"Shut up, Jayden. You don't know what you talking about. And talking won't help you right now anyway. Don't fuck with me. My patience is growing thin."

Traffic thickened even more due to the rush of people leaving New York. The slowing down of the vehicles made Madjesty angrier as she continued to steer the car. She had some place to be and she wanted to go quick.

"Wait...why is my leg wet?" Krazy asked looking down at his jeans.

"Hold up, my leg wet too," Tatio said.

"I told you I had to go to the bathroom," Jayden responded under her breath. "Should've let me piss."

Madjesty shook her head just as her phone rang. When she looked down at the screen, she looked annoyed. "Fuck!"

"It's bad?" Krazy asked.

"Yeah, let's do it at the next rest stop. I don't want to take any chances."

Jayden's eyes widened. She knew immediately that her life was about to change. So, she did what she normally did. Tried to talk her way out of the situation. "Okay, okay, Mad, can we talk now? Please." She began to hyperventilate. "You don't have to do whatever you're about to do. Please. We need to talk, please."

"About what?"

"Us."

"I'm listening."

"Okay, okay I know that we didn't have the best life. I know ma tried to tear us apart."

"She succeeded."

"I get that. And I know I could've been better. But...but...I never told you how I felt. I never admitted that it hurt me that, that you wanted to be the way you are, even after we learned who we were."

Madjesty frowned. "I don't know what you saying."

"When ma finally told us, we were girls instead of boys, I was relieved. And I didn't understand, I didn't get why you wanted to stay the same. And I hated you for it. I hated you for not being my sister. I hated you for—."

Mad knew that bringing up the past was a ploy, but she couldn't help but respond. "You think the way I am is a choice?"

"What you mean?"

"You think I wanna be something other than what I was born as?" Her voice raised. "Even after ma told me I was female; it didn't make a difference. I always knew in my heart I was male. So, saying what she said rolled off my shoulders. I don't even make people address me as 'he' no more. I just am what I am."

"But I think this is ma's fault. Had she not done this to you, then you wouldn't believe you are—"

"Fuck this got to do with what's going on now? Huh? At the end of the day I am male. In my heart...period." She slammed the steering wheel with a fist. "It don't have nothing to do with believing. It's fact, through and through. And what I'm telling you is that maybe, just maybe, ma being the lying bitch she was just coincided with who I was really born to be."

"Wait, you didn't know you were female when you were little, Mad?" Tatio asked.

"Why would you ask her some shit like that?" Krazy asked Tatio. "Huh?"

"Listen, Mad, whatever you about to do, you don't have to do it." Jayden said interrupting them. "Please."

"You gotta roll with the plan, Jayden. Because trust me. Things are about to change in your life whether you want it or not."

CHAPTER SIX

Madjesty pulled up in the rest stop and parked toward the back, where no other cars were present. "We have to hurry up." She pushed the gear shift up and exited the car. Krazy grabbed Jayden and Tatio exited too.

"Where are you taking me?" Jayden asked, in a heavy breath as she was dragged toward the back of the vehicle. Just then, a black large pickup rushed into the lot, and appeared to be on a hunt.

"Oh fuck, he's here." Krazy said just as Mad popped the trunk. "He gonna kill everybody."

"Hurry up!" She yelled.

Krazy shoved Jayden inside the trunk. "Oh my, God, Mad, please don't do this! I'm begging you!" When she tried to get out, Krazy stole her in the face and slid into the trunk with her right before Mad shoved it closed.

Within the darkness Krazy turned his phone on and she could see a gun aimed in her direction. "Listen, you gonna have to shut the fuck up." He whispered.

"Why? At least tell me what's going on."

"It ain't my place to tell you. But you gonna take this ride and you gonna be quiet while you do it."

She glared. "And if I don't?"

"Let's just say I'll have an excuse to shoot you in the face. And trust me, I've been knowing Mad for a long time now. The way you treat her, she'll definitely be in the mood to forgive me."

Madjesty walked over to the pick-up truck just as her father Kali and his friend Rex parked and stepped out of the vehicle in a hurry.

"Pops..." she said stuffing her hands in her pockets. "You good?"

"Mad, why did you do that?" He yelled throwing his hands up in the air. "Huh? What are you thinking?"

"Do what?"

"*Do what*?" He said louder. "Take my car...While I was on the side of the road?"

"I was just...I mean..."

He stepped closer. "You know where she is don't you?" He lowered his voice. "Tell me the truth. The last thing we want to do is lie to each other."

"Pops, I took the car because, because I didn't like what was popping off." She shrugged. "Just needed time to think. I mean I tried to tell you, but you didn't listen to me. Plus, I knew you could ride with Rex."

"That bitch will ruin your life, Mad." He pointed in her face. "And you trying to reach her before I do, won't stop what's gonna happen." He looked at his car. "Is Tatio inside?"

"Yeah. She went with me when we left." She tugged her cap. "Is Chink okay? He hit Jayden's van pretty hard."

"Yeah he fine." He sighed. "The cops were not too far behind him though when he hit it."

"What happen?"

"The cop asked what he hit, and he told him that the driver kept going." He paused. "After that we went into the woods looking for Jayden's van and she wasn't there. Just her driver. And he was dead. "

It was supposed to be simple.

After hiding in a hotel in New York while waiting on Jayden to finish the party, Kali got word she was leaving and driving back to Maryland. He set this up early, since he had April, one of Jayden's girl's helping to nudge her to take the drive instead of the flight so Kali could have at her.

Later that night, Kali was in his car with Mad and Tatio ready for war. Rex was driving his pick-up and Chink was in a van that would later hit Jayden's ride. Kali needed the extra cars so that when Chink made the hit, a pedestrian wouldn't slam in the back of him.

The moment Chink hit the van, causing it to push deep into the woods, Kali, Tatio and Mad piled out of Kali's car to find Jayden. And Rex pulled up in front of Chink's van. While searching, they got word that a police car was not too far away from the scene. So, they had to be quick. While Kali continued to check the woods, Mad used the opportunity to take her father's car. Kali was only a few minutes in when he heard cop's sirens, forcing him to suspend his search and jump into Rex's truck after realizing his was gone.

As planned, they left Chink to deal with the officer.

While driving her father's ride, Mad hit up Krazy who was also in the city to tell him where to meet her. She went up an exit and got back on the highway to see if Jayden would be walking on the side of the road.

She was.

And so, she got Jayden before he did.

Through it all, Mad had no idea that Kali had a tracker on his car. And so, he found his daughter at the rest stop. And he was heated. Dragging a hand down his face he said, "Get in the car, Mad."

When she entered his car, Kali got behind the wheel and adjusted the seat to its usual setting. Mad sat in the front and Tatio remained in the back. He put the car in gear and pulled out of the parking lot as Rex followed in the pick-up.

"Why did you leave me on the side of the road after Chink hit the van?" He said even though she answered already.

"Like I said I needed to get away." She looked down. "Plus, plus I knew you had a ride."

"She planned to have you killed, Mad." He looked at her while alternating his gaze on the road. "You do realize that, don't you? She planned to have me killed too. So, protecting her, even if she's your sister, is crazy."

"I don't believe she'd do that."

"Why not? You had half a million dollars that she deemed belonged to her. Plus, she was close to Rick. Closer than she was to you and her father. Do you really believe when he had you kidnapped that she wasn't involved? You smarter than this,

Kid. Don't let her fuck up our bond." He looked at her.

"I'll never let that happen."

"She can't mess up your bond." Tatio interjected, sliding forward in her seat. "Jayden is pretty but she's not you, sir. And Mad loves her dad. Plus, plus you're a better dad than my dad. Because—."

"Hold up, how do you know she's pretty?" Kali asked her through the rearview mirror. "You've never seen her before."

"Pops, leave her alone."

He glared at his daughter. "I asked her a question." He adjusted the mirror to see Tatio's face clearly while driving. "How do you know she's pretty?"

"She's pretty because she's, like, I mean, she's..." Tatio was becoming undone. It was just a matter of time before she spilled the beans and Mad knew it.

Kali sighed deeply. "Where is she?" He asked Tatio calmly. "Tell me where she is right now. Everything is okay."

Tatio looked at her friend. "Madjesty, I feel sick."

"Pull over on the shoulder, Pops." She begged. "Before she throws up."

"No, I want her to answer the question."

"Please. You know how she is...this is too much stress. I gotta get her together before she goes off and hurts herself."

"We don't have time for—."

"Please, Pops."

He sighed, dug in his pocket and tossed Mad his phone. "Text Rex that we pulling over a mile up." Madjesty complied and after a mile the vehicle immediately pulled over. Rex parked behind them.

Tatio quickly exited the car. Mad was on the way out until Kali grabbed her arm. "Are you lying to me?"

"Pops, I gotta check on her."

He released her. "Make it quick. I'ma call my wife to let her know I'm okay. But get her together. We have to head to the house next."

Jayden had been trembling ever since she heard Kali's voice in the trunk of the car. Still, she couldn't make out what was being said. The shine of the flashlight from Krazy's phone provided them with sight. Prior to hearing his baritone voice, the plan was to scream like crazy. Now she was glad she didn't. She was so nervous about what was happening, that she was on the verge of passing out. Krazy waving the gun in her face didn't help much.

"What did you do?" Krazy asked through clenched teeth inside the trunk. "Why are you so fucking evil?"

"I...I don't know what you talking about." She whispered. The front of her face was crusted with blood from being elbowed in the mouth and punched in the nose.

"You think you smarter than everybody don't you? After all this time you still think Madjesty is a puppet, right?"

"I never said that." Tears rolled down her face. "I...I never said that. I...I really don't know what I did to deserve all this. I care about my sister. And the last thing I want is us not to trust each other. She's all I have left in the world."

"Keep lying if you want. And I'll get out this trunk and let him know you in here. Because like

I said before, I already don't give a fuck about you. And Madjesty will be mad but she will—."

"Forgive you," Jayden sniffled. "And never forgive me. You already said that."

Kali was on the phone with his wife inside the car as Madjesty talked to Tatio outside. Vehicles continued to whiz up and down the road. "Listen, you're fine, we're fine."

"I know but I don't feel that way." She sobbed quietly, unable to catch a full breath. "I feel...I feel...I feel like he's going to find out she's in the trunk and be mad with me. I don't want him to be mad with me."

Madjesty grabbed her by the sides of the face. The brim of her cap almost stabbed her in the forehead. “Listen, he can never be mad with you. Never. You know why?”

Tatio continued to breathe heavily. “W...why?”

“Because I fuck with you. And anybody I fuck with, my father fucks with too.” She paused. “But listen...” She squeezed her face a little harder and stared into her eyes. “I need you to calm the fuck down. And I need you to know that everything will be okay. Because if you alert my father that my sister is in the trunk, he’s gonna go off and fuck up my plans. Okay?”

She nodded her head up and down.

“You gonna calm down?”

“Ye...yes.”

“You gonna play it cool?”

“Ye...yes.”

Madjesty kissed her on the forehead. “Good. Now let’s get back in the car.”

Kali was still on the phone with his wife when Madjesty and Tatio entered. He hung up and looked back at Tatio. “Let me ask you something, did you piss in my car?”

“No!” Madjesty interjected. “You, she, no…she didn’t pee in here.”

“Well something smells like urine.” He put the car in drive. “Guess I gotta go get it detailed.”

“Where we going now?” Mad said skipping the subject.

“Where you think? To her house.”

It was daybreak as Kali, Rex, Tatio and Madjesty sat inside of Jayden's house, as if they were invited guests. When too much time passed and she still wasn't home, Kali grew annoyed.

Standing up from the sofa he said, "This doesn't make sense." He placed his fists into his hips. "Something is way off."

"What you...what you mean, Pops?" Mad asked.

He stopped moving. "She said she was coming home." He looked around from where he sat. "April told me straight up. So, where the fuck is she? She definitely should have had a ride by now."

"I don't know." Her heart was rocking.

When he looked over at Tatio, she was trembling, so he focused on her a bit more. "What's wrong? No more games. Tell me what the fuck is going on."

"Nothing, Pops." Mad stood up. "She's nervous because you loud and—."

He raised his hand. "Let her talk."

"Pops, you know how she is. She has the mind of a fourteen-year-old." Mad persisted. "She ain't fit for all this yelling and shit. Let her—."

"Madjesty, how about you go outside for a minute and let your father talk to your friend in private." Rex said.

Mad's eyes widened. "But—."

"She gonna be fine." Rex continued. "Trust him." He placed a hand on her back and pushed her toward the foyer. "Go outside."

She took a deep breath and exited the house.

From the window she could see Rex sitting on one side of Tatio and her father sitting on the other. When Kali started rubbing her back with one hand, and Tatio started crying, Mad knew it was just a matter of time before Tatio told him that Jayden was in the trunk.

She needed to do something quickly. Luckily, she had his keys in her pocket.

CHAPTER SEVEN

Jayden and Krazy were in the trunk of the car lying on their sides, both wondering what was going on. "You know you snore right?" He asked.

"Well I'm tired. All of this stress is fucking with me. I'm still tired now."

"That's fine and all, except you have a serial killer looking for you. If you ask me, you're a little too comfortable."

"Well I'm still alive." She paused and held her stomach. "Although I have to shit now."

"If you do that, I will kill you." He aimed again. "Do you hear me?" He paused. "And I won't be able to—."

Suddenly the trunk popped open and a blast of air rushed inside. Mad's eyes were frantic and she looked afraid. "Tatio is about to tell him you're here! We have to get the fuck out of here. Now!"

Jayden and Krazy popped out of the trunk. When she saw where they were, her stomach dropped. "Wait, you're at my house?"

"Get the fuck in!" Krazy said.

When they were both inside, Madjesty jumped in the driver's seat and took off in Kali's car, just as they were running out.

Two hours later, they were still driving. Mad and Krazy found the tracker on the car earlier in the day and managed to tear it off. He had it there to track it against car thieves. While they took the hike, Jayden tried her best to stay awake, but the stress put her to sleep anyway.

When Krazy nudged her harshly, she was shocked to see that they were parked in front of a house made of wooden planks.

"You ready?" Krazy asked with a grin on his face.

She looked at Mad and then at him. "Where, where are we?"

"Let's go." Mad said softly.

When they entered the dwelling, Jayden was shocked to see two chairs on the floor sitting in front of the other. The scene looked stage and she was certain that this place had always been the destination.

"Sit down." Mad directed her calmly.

"What is this about?"

"This will be the last time I give you a direction. The next thing I'll do is hurt you. Badly. Now sit the fuck down."

Krazy walked up and stood behind Jayden. She looked at him and took a seat.

“Can you tell me what’s going on now? I’ve been more than patient,” she smiled, although she was afraid. “After all we are—.”

“Don’t.” Mad raised her hand. “I don’t want to hear we’re sisters again. The shit’s boring anyway.”

Jayden sighed deeply.

“Just so you know, my father wanted to kill you.” She shrugged. “Actually, I guess you know that much, considering you were laying in the back of his trunk. But I was like nah, I’m stepping in. I can’t let you kill my sister.” She paused. “So, let me ask you this, did you have Rick kidnap me and my son?”

“No, I—.”

Mad raised her hand, silencing her instantly. Reaching into her pocket, she made a call and placed it on speaker. "Derrick, I have her. Like I promised."

Jayden's eyes widened. Could that be her husband on the phone? Was that the reason he had been avoiding her all weekend? "Baby, is...is that you?"

"I'm here, Jayden." He said calmly.

"Derrick, you knew about this and you, and you let them take me?" Tears fell from her eyes.

"Listen to me, just listen." He said.

"Fuck that shit!" She yelled. "I have been going through hell all night. And now I find out that my husband knew about this?" She stabbed a fist into the palm of her hand.

"Just listen!" He yelled louder. "I know you're upset. But it was either you or our son. And I chose him."

Huge tears continued to run down her cheeks. "I can't believe this. I...I can't believe this is happening."

"This is your fault." He continued. "You wouldn't stop this obsession with your sister and Kali. You wouldn't stop trying to have him killed. But Madjesty promised me she's going to keep you safe. Isn't that right, Madjesty?"

Silence.

"Madjesty?" He said again.

She hung up and dropped the phone into her fatigues. "So, let me ask you again, were you in on kidnapping me and Cassius?" She clasped her hands together. "Did you know about it in advance?"

Jayden lowered her head. "I didn't, I didn't know they were going to take my nephew." She sniffled and looked up at her. "I knew about you being taken. I just, I just wanted you to feel what I felt when you took him from me."

Madjesty was so angry she was shivering. The truth finally revealed itself. "You know, earlier you asked about Cassius and I never answered you."

She nodded. "I...I know. How is he?"

"He didn't make it. After we left that place, he went to the hospital and died."

Jayden felt gut punched. Dizzy even. "I'm so sorry."

Madjesty got up and slapped her across the face with the back of her hand. Standing over top of her she said, "Didn't I tell you not to say you sorry again? Didn't I warn you?"

Up until that moment Mad was calm. Now the anger had revealed itself showcasing a monster. She was about to walk back to her seat when Jayden reached under her pants leg and removed the gun strapped to her ankle.

"I won't let you hurt me!" She yelled with the weapon trembling. And without hesitation she pulled the trigger. Instead of firing, it clicked. She pulled. It clicked again.

Mad was shocked. She tried to kill her once more.

Krazy placed a fist over his mouth and laughed into his hand. "I told you! I told you she would do that shit!" He paused. "Now can we kill this bitch and get it over with?"

Mad shook her head and looked at Jayden. "Krazy removed the bullets when you were sleep. On the way over here. He said you would try, and I didn't believe him. You proved me wrong."

Jayden's stomach rumbled and she dropped the weapon. "Please, please don't hurt me."

"You took from me in every way possible. And now you just tried to take my life. Why should I give you mercy?"

"Let's kill her, Mad." Krazy said. "Fuck the other shit. She may—."

Mad raised her hand. "You were so set on making our lives a fight. Making this about Madjesty vs. Jayden. When all I wanted was to love you. But I don't give a fuck anymore."

"Yes!" Krazy yelled. "About time!"

"But to me, killing you would be too easy." Mad nodded. "Killing you would be too quick."

"Mad, whatever you're about to do, I'm begging you not to." She cried real tears. "I was afraid, so I pulled the trigger."

"Bitch, you just tried to kill her! Why should she listen to anything you say?"

"Krazy, shut the fuck up!" Mad said, slamming her fist into her hand. "This about me and her."

"My bad." He looked down. "You right."

She focused back on Jayden. "Why shouldn't I hurt you? My son was in PICU until he died, because so much dirt covered his lungs he couldn't breathe. You've hunted my father nonstop. And now you try to kill me after I basically saved your life?"

Jayden cried softly for the first time in years. "I can't believe this is happening..."

"You will feel what being alone *really* feels like."

"Mad, let me, let me...okay let me explain."

"You even sent your first husband to murder my father. And when that failed, you killed him and then tried to solicit your new husband. But he was smarter and reached out to me instead."

Jayden finally understood that whatever was prepared for her, would be worse. "So, what are you going to do?" She sniffled and wiped her nose. "I don't care anymore."

Mad looked at Krazy who opened a door on the floor.

"I want you to experience what I experienced when I had to stay in a dirty hovel with my son. I want you to experience what it feels like to barely be able to breathe. And then, if you survive, I want you to experience the sexual abuse the women have felt who work for you. To experience what I went through when I was raped."

Krazy grabbed his dick and grinned. He was hard.

"Mad, please...I...I'm hurt." She raised her shirt. "Can't you see?"

"Nah, had you patched up remember? You'll survive. I survived much worse."

Krazy lifted Jayden up kicking and screaming and tossed her in the hole. No stairs were present, so she fell hard on a set of pillows. It immediately knocked the wind out of her lungs. "Fuuuuuccccckkk!" She rubbed her throbbing back.

Madjesty stood next to Krazy. "You're going to stay here. And it won't be easy. At some point I will return. If I see who I see now, I will kill you. If I see a change, the next part of your torture will begin. And then maybe you will live."

"Mad, please...I'm your fucking sister!"

"You reap what you sew. I hope what you sewed fits."

They closed the door and walked out the shed.

The next morning Mad walked into Kali's kitchen in Upper Marlboro, Maryland. He was just about to eat breakfast when she entered. Life for Kali had changed somewhat. He was married to a cute young girl named Swalazy from Africa, and Mad liked her a lot. Mainly because unlike his ex,

Antionette, she stayed out the business and let the family be. She wasn't intimidated by their bond and embraced it.

"Hey, sweetheart, are you hungry?" Swalazy asked before kissing Mad on the cheek.

"No, I'm good." She sat down and tugged on her baseball cap. Her red dreads hung heavily on her shoulders.

"Eat something." Kali said firmly. "It's been a long night."

Swalazy smiled at her husband and fixed Mad a plate of grits, bacon and eggs. Afterwards she winked at them and walked out.

Kali ate in silence for five minutes before placing his fork down and running his hand down his face. "Where the keys to my car?"

She slid them over. "To be old that car rides smoothly." She said, trying to crack a joke. "Like a Benz but older."

He glared. “You hurt me. I feel betrayed.”

She didn’t know what she expected him to say, but it definitely wasn’t that. Hearing that she hurt her father was the last thing she wanted. And at the same time, she couldn’t deny its merit. “I needed to do this my way, Pops.”

“She will manipulate you.”

“I won’t let that happen.”

“You already have.” He paused. “She made five attempts on your life, Mad. And many more on mine.”

“We don’t have any proof she tried to kill me. I mean, she, she…” Mad heard herself and knew she sounded ridiculous. Jayden was all things evil. “You’re right. But if I do this, and I will kill her if I have to, I need to know that my sister ain’t there no more first. I need to know she can’t be changed. If not, I’ll be killing the only family I have left.”

“You got me.”

"I know, Pops. And I love you for it. But just...just let me do this."

"Why though?" He threw his arms up. "I don't get this shit."

Mad sat back and leaned to the right. "I've begged for death before. I wanted life to be taken from me. When I was being raped. And when I heard my son cry while we were about to be buried alive." She sighed. "And definitely after his death." She shook her head slowly. "I think of wanting to die now." She whispered. "That's how I know that killing someone is too easy. People beg to die every day, Pops. But no one wants to be tortured. No one wants to be forced to listen to their own thoughts." She pointed at her head. "To have to remember that the things you did in life brought you to that dark moment." She sighed. "Jayden hasn't suffered enough in life. She's spoiled. I wanna change that. In the process, I want to see if she's worth saving. And it won't be easy for her. It won't be easy for me."

He finally understood. "I'll give you two months. And if you don't see what you're looking for, promise me you'll come to me. So that I can kill her for you. I know you won't be able to do this yourself."

"I will do what—."

"I'm saying if you can't!" He interrupted. "Because we can't leave her in the world, son. We can't leave her alive after she goes through this level of mental warfare. She's too dangerous. And I won't have that."

Mad grabbed her fork even though her stomach churned, and she wasn't hungry. "If I can't, I will call you."

"Promise me."

Mad sighed deeply. Since she and Kali entered the new phase of their lives, as adults, they took promises seriously. So, making a promise was major. “If I can’t kill her, and it’s time, I’ll come to you. I *promise.*”

He leaned back and smiled. “Well…let the countdown begin.”

COMING SOON

The Cartel Publications Order Form

www.thecartelpublications.com

Inmates **ONLY** receive novels for $10.00 per book **PLUS** shipping fee **PER BOOK.**
(Mail Order **MUST** come from inmate directly to receive discount)

Title		Price
Shyt List 1	________	$15.00
Shyt List 2	________	$15.00
Shyt List 3	________	$15.00
Shyt List 4	________	$15.00
Shyt List 5	________	$15.00
Shyt List 6	________	$15.00
Pitbulls In A Skirt	________	$15.00
Pitbulls In A Skirt 2	________	$15.00
Pitbulls In A Skirt 3	________	$15.00
Pitbulls In A Skirt 4	________	$15.00
Pitbulls In A Skirt 5	________	$15.00
Victoria's Secret	________	$15.00
Poison 1	________	$15.00
Poison 2	________	$15.00
Hell Razor Honeys	________	$15.00
Hell Razor Honeys 2	________	$15.00
A Hustler's Son	________	$15.00
A Hustler's Son 2	________	$15.00
Black and Ugly	________	$15.00
Black and Ugly As Ever	________	$15.00
Ms Wayne & The Queens of DC **(LGBT)**	________	$15.00
Black And The Ugliest	________	$15.00
Year Of The Crackmom	________	$15.00
Deadheads	________	$15.00
The Face That Launched A Thousand Bullets	________	$15.00
The Unusual Suspects	________	$15.00
Paid In Blood	________	$15.00
Raunchy	________	$15.00
Raunchy 2	________	$15.00
Raunchy 3	________	$15.00
Mad Maxxx (4th Book Raunchy Series)	________	$15.00
Quita's Dayscare Center	________	$15.00
Quita's Dayscare Center 2	________	$15.00
Pretty Kings	________	$15.00
Pretty Kings 2	________	$15.00
Pretty Kings 3	________	$15.00
Pretty Kings 4	________	$15.00
Silence Of The Nine	________	$15.00
Silence Of The Nine 2	________	$15.00
Silence Of The Nine 3	________	$15.00

Prison Throne	____________	$15.00
Drunk & Hot Girls	____________	$15.00
Hersband Material **(LGBT)**	____________	$15.00
The End: How To Write A Bestselling Novel In 30 Days (Non-Fiction Guide)	____________	$15.00
Upscale Kittens	____________	$15.00
Wake & Bake Boys	____________	$15.00
Young & Dumb	____________	$15.00
Young & Dumb 2: Vyce's Getback	____________	$15.00
Tranny 911 **(LGBT)**	____________	$15.00
Tranny 911: Dixie's Rise **(LGBT)**	____________	$15.00
First Comes Love, Then Comes Murder	____________	$15.00
Luxury Tax	____________	$15.00
The Lying King	____________	$15.00
Crazy Kind Of Love	____________	$15.00
Goon	____________	$15.00
And They Call Me God	____________	$15.00
The Ungrateful Bastards	____________	$15.00
Lipstick Dom **(LGBT)**	____________	$15.00
A School of Dolls **(LGBT)**	____________	$15.00
Hoetic Justice	____________	$15.00
KALI: Raunchy Relived (5th Book in Raunchy Series)	____________	$15.00
Skeezers	____________	$15.00
Skeezers 2	____________	$15.00
You Kissed Me, Now I Own You	____________	$15.00
Nefarious	____________	$15.00
Redbone 3: The Rise of The Fold	____________	$15.00
The Fold (4th Redbone Book)	____________	$15.00
Clown Niggas	____________	$15.00
The One You Shouldn't Trust	____________	$15.00
The WHORE The Wind Blew My Way	____________	$15.00
She Brings The Worst Kind	____________	$15.00
The House That Crack Built	____________	$15.00
The House That Crack Built 2	____________	$15.00
The House That Crack Built 3	____________	$15.00
The House That Crack Built 4	____________	$15.00
Level Up **(LGBT)**	____________	$15.00
Villains: It's Savage Season	____________	$15.00
Gay For My Bae	____________	$15.00
War	____________	$15.00
War 2: All Hell Breaks Loose	____________	$15.00
War 3: The Land Of The Lou's	____________	$15.00
War 4: Skull Island	____________	$15.00
War 5: Karma	____________	$15.00
War 6: Envy	____________	$15.00
War 7: Pink Cotton	____________	$15.00
Madjesty vs. Jayden (Novella)	____________	$8.99
You Left Me No Choice	____________	$15.00

(**Redbone 1** & **2** are **NOT** Cartel Publications novels and if **ordered** the cost is **FULL** price of $15.00 **each**. **No Exceptions**.)

Please add **$5.00** for shipping and handling fees for up to **(2) BOOKS PER ORDER**. (INMATES INCLUDED) (See next page for details)

The Cartel Publications * P.O. BOX 486 OWINGS MILLS MD 21117

Name: ______________________________

Address: ______________________________

City/State: ______________________________

Contact/Email: ______________________________

Please allow 8-10 BUSINESS days Before shipping.

****PLEASE NOTE DUE TO COVID-19 SOME ORDERS MAY TAKE UP TO 3 WEEKS BEFORE THEY SHIP****

The Cartel Publications is NOT responsible for Prison Orders rejected!

NO RETURNS and NO REFUNDS
NO PERSONAL CHECKS ACCEPTED
STAMPS NO LONGER ACCEPTED